HOPSCOTCH
TWISTY TALES

Sleeping Beauty– 100 Years Later

by Laura North and Gary Northfield

FRANKLIN WATTS
LONDON•SYDNEY

This story is based on the traditional fairy tale,
Sleeping Beauty, but with a new twist.
You can read the original story in
Hopscotch Fairy Tales. Can you make
up your own twist for the story?

First published in 2010 by
Franklin Watts
338 Euston Road
London
NW1 3BH

Franklin Watts Australia
Level 17/207 Kent Street
Sydney, NSW 2000

Text © Laura North 2010
Illustrations © Gary Northfield 2010

A CIP catalogue record for this book is available
from the British Library.

ISBN 978 14451 0180 4 (hbk)
ISBN 978 14451 0186 6 (pbk)

Series Editor: Melanie Palmer
Series Advisor: Catherine Glavina
Series Designer: Peter Scoulding

Printed in China

Franklin Watts is a division of
Hachette Children's Books,
an Hachette UK company
www.hachette.co.uk

For Paul – L.N.

A long time ago,
a King and Queen had
a beautiful baby daughter.

"Let's have a big party to celebrate," said the King. They invited everyone in the kingdom.

But they forgot to invite
one fairy.

She burst into the party in a rage. "I curse your daughter! She will cut her finger and fall asleep for a hundred years. Only a prince can wake her!"

"That will teach them to forget me!"
she thought as she flew away.

The King and Queen were terrified.
"No sharp things!" screamed
the Queen, taking the knife
and fork away.

"No playing outdoors!" said the King. The Princess wasn't allowed to do anything. She was miserable.

When the Princess reached her 18th birthday, the King and Queen let her wander round the castle.

She found a room with an old
spinning wheel.

The Princess was curious.

She tried making some thread

on the spinning wheel.

"Ouch!" she cried. She had pricked her finger on the needle. Suddenly, she fell into a deep sleep.

Everyone else fell asleep, too!
Years passed. Cobwebs
covered the castle.

One hundred years
later, a Prince wearing
sunglasses drove up to the castle.

He talked on a mobile phone.
He listened to music in earphones.
He wore jeans. A lot had changed
while the Princess had been asleep!

The Prince found the Princess.
"What a sleeping beauty!" he
thought. He went over to kiss her.

"Are you my Prince, my true love?"
asked the Princess, waking up.
"Just call me Harry," said the Prince.
"I'd like to take you on a date."

"A date?" said the Princess,
"I wonder what that is!"
Harry took her outside.
Everything looked so different!

"Is this your carriage? Where is the horse?" asked the Princess. "No need for one of those!" said Harry, starting the car engine.

"Let's go to the funfair," Harry said.
The Princess whizzed around and
upside down on a rollercoaster.
"I've never had so much fun!"
she screamed.

Harry gave her a single red rose.

A thorn on the rose cut her finger.

"Oh no, what will happen to me now?" cried the Princess. "Will I fall asleep for another 100 years?"

"No, here's a plaster," said Harry and he stuck it on her finger.

The Princess smiled. Life was so much better 100 years later!

Puzzle 1

Put these pictures in the correct order.
Which event do you think is most important?
Now try writing the story in your own words!

Puzzle 2

Choose the correct speech bubbles for each character. Can you think of any others? Turn over to find the answers.

Answers

Puzzle 1

The correct order is: 1e, 2d, 3f, 4a, 5c, 6b

Puzzle 2

The Princess: 1, 4

Harry: 2, 5

The bad fairy: 3, 6

Look out for more Hopscotch Twisty Tales and Fairy Tales:

TWISTY TALES

The Three Little Pigs and the New Neighbour
ISBN 978 1 4451 0175 0*
ISBN 978 1 4451 0181 1

Jack and the Bean Pie
ISBN 978 1 4451 0176 7*
ISBN 978 1 4451 0182 8

Brownilocks and the Three Bowls of Cornflakes
ISBN 978 1 4451 0177 4*
ISBN 978 1 4451 0183 5

Cinderella's Big Foot
ISBN 978 1 4451 0178 1*
ISBN 978 1 4451 0184 2

Little Bad Riding Hood
ISBN 978 1 4451 0179 8*
ISBN 978 1 4451 0185 9

**Sleeping Beauty –
100 Years Later**
ISBN 978 1 4451 0180 4*
ISBN 978 1 4451 0186 6

FAIRY TALES

The Three Little Pigs
ISBN 978 0 7496 7905 7

Little Red Riding Hood
ISBN 978 0 7496 7901 9*
ISBN 978 0 7496 7907 1

Goldilocks and the Three Bears
ISBN 978 0 7496 7903 3

Hansel and Gretel
ISBN 978 0 7496 7904 0

Rapunzel
ISBN 978 0 7496 7900 2*
ISBN 978 0 7496 7906 4

Rumpelstiltskin
ISBN 978 0 7496 7902 6*
ISBN 978 0 7496 7908 8

The Elves and the Shoemaker
ISBN 978 0 7496 8543 0

The Ugly Duckling
ISBN 978 0 7496 8538 6*
ISBN 978 0 7496 8544 7

Sleeping Beauty
ISBN 978 0 7496 8545 4

The Frog Prince
ISBN 978 0 7496 8540 9*
ISBN 978 0 7496 8546 1

The Princess and the Pea
ISBN 978 0 7496 8541 6*
ISBN 978 0 7496 8547 8

Dick Whittington
ISBN 978 0 7496 8542 3*
ISBN 978 0 7496 8548 5

Cinderella
ISBN 978 0 7496 7417 5

Snow White and the Seven Dwarfs
ISBN 978 0 7496 7418 2

The Pied Piper of Hamelin
ISBN 978 0 7496 7419 9

Jack and the Beanstalk
ISBN 978 0 7496 7422 9

The Three Billy Goats Gruff
ISBN 978 0 7496 7420 5

The Emperor's New Clothes
ISBN 978 0 7496 7421 2